Real Passions Real Love

Erotic Poems and Stories

Iris and Ian

ISBN-13: 9798798191024
ISBN-10: 1477123456

Cover design by: Art Painter
Library of Congress Control Number: 2018675309
Printed in the United States of America

To Ian From Iris, and from Iris to Ian

"In love there are two things: bodies and words."
JOYCE CAROL OATES

Contents

Beneath Me

Beneath me is your naked body,
In all its sensuousness.
It is slowly slithering and quivering,
In total sexual excess.

Move and I move too,
As we undulate as one,
As we slowly abdicate,
Ourselves for the one.

Beneath my cupped hands,
Are your naked breasts,
Gently I will squeeze them,
Until they plead conquest.

Move and I move too,
As I hear your sighs,
As your heart takes wing,
And journeys to the skies.

Beneath me is all desire,
That heaven can ever hold,
All that may be experienced
That is more valuable than gold.

Move and I move too,
In unison and more,

Our passion has no limits,
It is all I could ever wish for.

There is Love

There is love
and there is desire;
Each is owed
It's own kind of fire.

Me Tarzan

Me Tarzan, you Jane.

You brushed by me
and you let your hair
touch my nostrils again.

I told you what that does to me;
I can't be held responsible
for my behavior then.

I start to growl and change.
Primal urges come up in me
and I am part lion and part ape again:
The smell of the jungle arrives,
there is lush high grass and flies,
I can feel the African heat,
and I am part of the veldt again.

I pounce, I mate.

Me Tarzan, you Jane

Still Dark

It was still dark
when I stirred out of sleep
the morning after a night
of passion and pleasure.

You were lying next to me
on your side
and just atop of my arm.
Your back was to me.

I stared at your body
that was half covered
and half exposed
in all its naked loveliness.

The faint remembrances
of the night before
ran through my head,
my heart and through my loins.

I must have stared at you
for over half an hour
before getting closer
and touching you,
allowing the dream
to become reality
again.

A Coyote's Song

A coyote took a mate,
who was lean and swift,
and also was a beauty;
When he lay down at her side
it was out of sincere love,
not primal need or duty.

"Oh, lick my paws, nose and face,"
her coyote yowl begs,
"Then thrust it through, strong into,
the center of my hind legs."

He met her near a small creek bed
one warm summer night,
when she was washing there;
He saw she had perfect claws,
a long, even nose
and red-tinged, short-cropped hair

"Oh, lick my paws, nose and face,"
her coyote yowl begs,
"Then thrust it through, strong into,
the center of my hind legs."

She was coming in from her daily swim,
at around midnight,
all dripping wet and glistening,
Crowded though the creek bed was,

they only heard the other panting,
and they weren't even listening.

"Oh, lick my paws, nose and face,"
her coyote yowl begs,
"Then thrust it through, strong into,
the center of my hind legs."

They wore two happy morning smiles,
after they howled together in the night,
allowing no one to get their sleep;
Because they danced all around,
Back and forth, and up and down,
before collapsing in a wet fur heap.

"Oh, lick my paws, nose and face,"
her coyote yowl begs,
"Then thrust it through, strong into,
the center of my hind legs."

Newspaper

You seem so engrossed
when you read
your morning paper.

One morning
I will make love to you
when you're so engaged!

I'll let you start.
Then, while you're reading,
"Most political experts. . . ."
--I'll slip your blouse off.
Since you haven't noticed
anything wrong,
I'll continue undressing you.

While you read the story of,
"The fall general election . . . ."
--off will come your pants!
Next to fall will be your bra,
while you read,
"The ballot initiatives . . . ."
Then, quickly, your panties will pass
right over your legs!

As you read, "Of all the Propositions . . . ."
-- I'll let my tongue slip

from your stomach
to your breast
and back down again.
You'll go on, as you always do,
and just read,
"Most Californians believe. . . ."
--as my hands move up and down
and all around again, again and again!

I'll be licking at your pussy
as you read,
"The initiative's ban . . . ."
and you will be enthralled,
and not know exactly why,
believing it was just a lively,
lively story line.

As you read the line,
"The alternative party wants. . . ."
I, unbuckling my pants,
will prepare to enter you.
"The situation in Geneva . . . ."
is on your mind, but
I'm inside of you!

A Hunger

When we kiss I feel a hunger
to have you closer, dear,
a bold, exploding hunger
to always have you near.
I crave your searching fingers
when they crawl all over me,
your probing, caressing fingers
on my cheeks, my mouth, my knee.

My hand searches for your limbs,
to feel the warmth of your skin,
I have waited far too long
for this moment to begin.
I want it to be extended,
not quick, savage and rough.
But my hungry is so huge,
and time never seems enough.

I want to feel your warm, wet mouth
brushing and crushing against mine,
feel our tongues dart and probe
so much that they entwine.
I want to explore your velvet skin,
trace the lines of limbs far-flung,
and taste the route from breast to belly
with my slow-moving tongue.

Where are all your secret places?

Invite me in, I do no harm.
Let my mouth search and inspect them
to excite and to make them warm.
I want to thrust my dick in you
and screw with abandonment;
I want you to feel in places new,
and come until you're ably spent!

The Feast

*T*here you are. You're leaning over and resting your arms on the island counter in the kitchen as I prepare the feast. You watch me as I cut, dice and portion our food, and . . . I watch you.

The top of your blouse falls open slightly as you lean. I view just the top rounded edges of your breasts and a small portion of your bra. It's red, bright red! I wonder if your panties are red as well. I wonder what they may look like. Are they thong style? I want to think so.

You ask if you could help in some way. I say, "Yes, please set the table."

You start placing the dishes and the flatware at our spots on the table. I see your behind. You have beautiful buttocks, nicely and delicately curved. Your butt is softly outlined by your loose pants. I can make out, I think, the panty lines made by your red panties (or at least I want them to be red).

You move from side to side and your butt jiggles just slightly, temptingly. You stretch and your butt beckons, "Enter me, enter me." I continue cutting, dicing and . . . thinking.

You finish setting the table and come over to the counter again. You laugh at a remark I make and your face tilts upward and your eyes roll. I have seen your face that way while we're making love. I picture you that way again, with you on top of me: Your head is tilted back and it's moving from side to side, your hand is up, palm out, covering your mouth, and your eyes are rolling. I see you that way and I can hear you sigh and moan as well.

You're talking now. You are telling me about your daughter. You laugh and I see you smile. Your mouth opens. Oh, how I want to put my cock in your mouth! I see your tongue. It has licked my cock so lovingly, and I want it there again. Now, I want it there now, but -- I go on cutting, dicing and . . . thinking.

I realize you're paying attention to how I'm looking at you. You ask me if there's something wrong. I mumble something about the sauce I am beginning to make: It isn't coming out as I want it to. "Do you like cream sauces?" I ask you. You don't realize what I'm really alluding to. I concentrate on the sauce now and . . . continue to think.

I look at you. You're sitting there at the counter now with a glass of wine in your hand. You take a drink. In my mind's eye I see you naked, with your legs crossed. I imagine those legs crossed over head, and my face buried in your crotch. I slide the tip of my tongue over the roof of my mouth and pretend that it's your clitoris. I move my tongue up and down, back and forth, up and down, and back and forth. I can almost taste you: A sweet-salty nectar that is unlike anything I've ever tasted. I go back to my sauce. It should be bottled, that taste of yours: *Chateau D'Joan*. I smile.

You are still talking, about your daughter-in-law now, when I tell you that everything is ready. I have already ravished and devoured you in my mind. Yet, we have not eaten. I think to myself, it's like having my dessert first, then my entree.

I smile. You look at me with a quizzical expression, as if to ask, what are you thinking about? I just continue to smile.

Ask Me

Ask me to make love to you on the street and I will take your hand to my mouth, press my tongue on your palm and slowly and sensuously lick it.

Ask me to make love to you in a supermarket checkout line and I will put my hand in the back pocket of your jeans while I kiss the back of your neck.

Ask me to make love to you in a restaurant and I will take the half tomato from your salad, drizzle a small amount of oil on it and then explore the indentations and clefts of it with my tongue, sucking and devouring it with my lips only.

Ask me to make love with you in a movie theater and I will put my sweater on your lap, and my hand underneath the sweater. Then I will slowly, very, very slowly move my hand up, around and under your clothes till it reaches your cunt. I will then touch, tease and entice it until it trembles and vibrates.

Ask me to make love to you in my dreams and I will carry you to a lush meadow at daybreak, the mist still clinging to the ground and spread you among clover and lilac, the moon over your shoulder and the sun rising over my back. I will place fragrant blossoms all around you to mingle with the pine scent of the forest, climb on top of you and then exhort you to breath the wilderness air with me as you've never done before.

Nothing

Nothing is better
than the feeling
of how it feels
to lie next to you
hearing earth sounds
in the dark of night.
--Except the sight of your naked skin
as you're walking straight towards me
white skin outlined in pale moonlight.

At A Table

At a table eating dinner tonight,
--were we at at that new Italian place?
My eyes went blind,
Wanting you so much,
In my longing body,
And in my lustful mind.

I wanted to say salacious things,
And have your pussy reply to me:
How it yearns to capture,
All the sperm I send to thee.

Limerick # 1

There once was a lady from Poway,
Who always left men in her driveway,
It was okay most of the time,
A peck on the cheek was fine,
Fucking them there? --what would the neighbors say!

Limerick # 2

There once was a randy blond nurse,
Who liked looking at cocks in reverse,
She liked size the most,
But wasn't opposed,
To cocks that went in transverse.

The Golden One

My tongue hovers over it,
The Golden One,
on this hot, sultry night
that smells of fire,
and your scent,
after we found ourselves
On the stair
looking at each other
with longing desire
and then gave ourselves
to the urge of lust.

My mouth moves across
your thrusting cunt,
The Golden One,
as I delicately touch and hunt
each part of it with my tongue
and you react with joy
and longing, hungry sounds.
We play and caress each other,
hands everywhere,
fingers touching and teasing,
lovingly pleasing,
amazing ourselves
with each other's touch;
Touch that is loving and hard,

delicate and rough,
sweet and furious,
kind and engagingly tough.

The wind is still violent outside.
Has it stirred us?
Has it fanned our passion?
The hunger and itch was there,
perhaps it just set the scene.

You

I first met you
As a man meets someone new,
Between the necessities of life
And the primal dance of woo.
But you were quite unique
And I was thoroughly piqued
By the sense that you engaged my brain
And my earthy urge to screw.

Now the courtship starts
The time of dueling hearts,
When different lives get sorted out
Or one of us departs.
It isn't all that hard,
As long as you drop your guard,
And try to find a way
To forget that you've been scarred.

The Museum

He had received an invitation to the opening of the new museum, but really didn't want to go. His best friend Bill was an active member of the museum association and had talked him into going.

Bill said, "Hey, please go. My wife is going to be talking to her friends the entire night and I need someone there I know I can talk to." So he thought he would show up and stay awhile for his friend. It was a black tie event, so he broke out his tuxedo and bow tie for the ball.

He had just arrived, and was looking for his friend, when he saw her across the hall talking to someone near the bar. He couldn't keep his eyes off her. He believed her to be one of the most beautiful women he had ever seen.

Her hair was done up elegantly behind her, showing off her sleek neck. She wore a long shiny black silk gown that fit her wonderful figure perfectly. He couldn't help but notice the spaghetti straps that shone her smooth shoulders and the slight slit up the dress that allowed the single profile of a leg to peek through.

Her beauty mesmerized him. He couldn't help staring at her. But, then he noticed that she too was staring at him. She was trying to concentrate on her conversation with her friend but couldn't. She saw him staring at her, and tried to be coy, but couldn't help taking numerous looks back at him.

He was a very striking man. Dark hair and good build, with eyes that seemed to take her breath away. His tuxedo fit him nicely, allowing her imagination to run away with what was underneath it. All thought of the conversation she was having with her friend seemed to have disappeared.

All he could think about was how he should not let this opportunity get away. She didn't appear to be with anyone, so he thought he had a chance. He approached her, unable to look away from her exceptional eyes. He could smell her fragrant perfume emanating from her as he approached closer.

She smelled his masculine cologne as his deep smooth voice asked her to dance. Her heart was in her throat, unable to speak, all she could do was allow him to take her arm, as he led her to the dance floor.

They seemed to dance as one to the orchestra's music. They glided across the floor, not noticing the other dancers, but being noticed by them. They were entranced with each other; Nothing else seemed to matter then. Time and space stood still while they were lost within their own thoughts and conversation. His wit made her smile, allowing him to see how much more beautiful she was when she did smile. Her charm made him grin, allowing her to see the sparkle in his eyes.

They both would have sworn that they had only been on the dance floor for only a short while, though in reality it had been all night. They hadn't taken a break, but they weren't tired. They hadn't gotten a drink, but they weren't thirsty. They were just lost within each other.

The orchestra had stopped playing moments earlier, but they hadn't stopped dancing. It wasn't till the orchestra began to break down their equipment that they noticed the night had come to an end. They looked at each other and began to laugh.

He leaned forward, thanking her for a wonderful time, and kissed her on the cheek. As he pulled back they could see it in each other's eyes, the want, the need, for more.

He leaned forward again and kissed her on the mouth. His mouth enfolding hers, as she slightly parted her lips. Their tongues reaching out to the other, passion and craving mingled together as they touched. His kiss was as deep and passionate as his voice. Her's was as soft and romantic as her smile.

His lips pressed against hers, their tongues continuing to crave the company of the other, as they lightly stroked each other. He slowly began to deeply search her mouth, reaching deep within hers, continuing to flick its way through her mouth, as she began to loose control of her tongue. His inflamed passionate kiss continued, submerged in her mouth, his tongue playing with hers, sending excitement and desire through her body, each nerve sensitive to the touch. He pulled his mouth away and looked into her closed eyes. Once again time and space had seemed to stop for them.

She opened her eyes slowly, then looked around the room. She looked back at him, a slight look of shock on her face. "I'm so sorry, but I have to go. Sorry," She said.

He reached into his breast pocket and pulled out a card and pen. He wrote down his phone number. "It's OK, really. Here's my number, please call me?" He said as he handed her the card. And then she left. Looking back one last time at him as she left the building, he watched her leave and felt an enormous sense of emotion come over him. What was that old saying, love at first sight? He had never believed it until now.

She called him the next day and they talked for hours. They talked about each other, trying to get to know one another. They talked into the night until they both decided that they needed to get some sleep. The next night he called her.

They talked to each other every night that week, from the time they got home till the time they went to bed. Just general things at first, then more specific as the week went on. They were beginning to get to know one another inside and out.

That Thursday when he returned home from work he changed from his suit and tie to a dark blue silk shirt and gray slacks. He got ready to call her and see if she would like to do something that night. He tried the number, but there was no answer. He tried again, thinking that he might have mis-dialed, but yet there was still no answer. He didn't know what to do; he seemed lost.

He was just about ready to head back to his bedroom and change again, when there was a knock at the door. When he answered it his heart jumped with excitement. There she was!

She stood in the doorway wearing black high heels, silky black stockings running up her shapely legs and a short black mini skirt, allowing him to view her legs. A dark gray blouse that was off the shoulders flattered her, as did her hair which was swept upward in a French curl with cascading soft silky ringlets. Her beauty shocked him; he couldn't speak, so he had to motion her in, instead of asking.

"I was in the area, so I thought I might drop by. I hope you don't mind?"

He finally gained control of himself, and grabbed her arm as she was passing by him. He turned her around and kissed her. His lips pressed against hers as she willingly allowed his tongue to penetrate deep within her mouth. Intense, passionate, he held her there with his kiss for several moments. Once his mouth released hers, they stood there looking at each other.

He finally broke the spell; "I was just trying to call you. I was going to ask if you would like to go to dinner and maybe a movie, or something."

"May I use your bathroom?" She asked.

"Sure, it's right in there." He said as he pointed the way.

A few moments later she came out of the bathroom and stood next to the doorway wearing only a black lacy see-through bra without shoulder straps, black lacy panties, a black garter belt attached to her silky stockings, and her high heel shoes. "Going out? I was thinking of something else." she said.

When he turned around to look at her he was taken aback by her beauty and sexiness. He could feel an arousal in his groin slowly growing and inflaming.

He walked straight towards her and picked her up in his arms and kissed her. He carried her off in his arms to the bedroom. Never letting the kiss go as he held her in his arms. She could feel him growing hard against her as he carried her to the bedroom.

He laid her carefully on top of the bed. She began to unbutton his silk shirt while she kicked off her shoes. She removed his shirt and lightly caressed his bare chest. He leaned forward and began to delicately kiss her neck as he removed his own shoes, kicking them next to hers. He lay down beside her as he gently nibbled her ear and neck. He continued to suckle and nibble as he began undoing her bra, releasing her attractive breasts. She lightly caressed and gently scratched his back.

He kissed his way down to her breasts, picking out one, then engulfed the nipple with his mouth, lightly sucking. He then began to flick the nipple lightly with his tongue. He could feel it growing taunt between his lips, as he then softly nibbled upon it, causing her to quietly moan. He then moved over to the other, neglected breast, and repeated the procedure, causing her to moan again.

She reached down and undid his pants, tenderly touching his cock through his underwear. He pulled himself back, unexpectedly to her touch. He removed his pants and socks, wearing only his jockey shorts now.

He then brought his mouth down to her belly, carefully licked and kissed around the navel with his tongue.

He sat up and unclipped her stockings from her garter. Then, slowly, one at a time, he removed her stockings from her enticing legs, every now and then leaning over to lightly kiss her leg. He then removed her garter belt, once again leaning forward and kissing her belly every so often. Then, slowly again, he removed her lacy panties. To his wonderful surprise, he noticed that she was completely shaven.

She quickly sat up and helped him remove his jockey shorts, allowing his now throbbing cock to be released. She pushed him down upon the bed, then firmly grasped his hardened cock, feeling it pulsate in her hand. She leaned forward and softly kissed the top of it.

He maneuvered her body on top of his, positioning her moistness right above his mouth, as she slowly engulfed his cock within her mouth. He moaned slightly as he pulled her down on top of him, opening his mouth to welcome her.
She could feel his cock pulsate within her mouth as she rolled her tongue around him. She slightly moaned with him in her mouth as she felt him begin to lick around the outside of her moistness. He slowly opened her up with his tongue as he sought his way to her clitoris. She moaned more while she was drawing back on his cock with her mouth.

He found her clitoris and lightly touched it with his tongue, causing her to slowly rotate her hips, while she continued to suck his cock. He continued to lightly touch and flick his tongue about inside her, causing her breathing to quicken, as she continuously moved her mouth up and down his quaking cock, attempting to take him further into her mouth each time. His tongue worked wildly within her and she began to softly shake.

She couldn't hold him in her mouth any longer, her body was shuddering so, and let him go, releasing a loud moan deep from within herself. He maneuvered his way behind her as her body slightly trembled on all fours, on the edge of her first orgasm. He then, from behind her, slowly penetrated her. She gasped for breath as she felt him enter her. He moved inward slowly, pushing himself forward into her, until she had taken all of him. He then slowly withdrew himself, as her moans grew.

Once he had almost completely withdrawn himself, he slammed himself into her quickly, causing her to gasp and moan loudly. He then began pounding into her ferociously, yet carefully, turning her breathing into a quick pant, and causing her to moan uncontrollably. He continued to thrust into her, faster, harder, deeper, as she wildly shook her head back and forth, trying to move herself to the same rhythm, attempting to take him further into herself. He could feel her body tremble as she began to scream. Her orgasm causing her to shake, yet he persisted on his actions, yet now with more intent.

As her buttock was becoming painfully red from the wonderful beating it was taking, he slowly withdrew himself. Exhausted from his actions, but not yet completing his task, he lay down beside her. She looked over at him and noticed his throbbing cock, still pulsating, daring her.

She moved atop him and slowly mounted him while looking into his eyes. She continued to look into his eyes as she rode him slowly at first, but gradually picking up the pace, grinning from atop him. He reached up and delicately massaged her breasts as she gyrated her hips faster. She then leaned toward his chest, panting once again, continuing to ride his throbbing member, but feeling herself on the verge of orgasm again.

He leaned forward and kissed her, as he began to assist her in the thrusting, raising her slightly off the bed. He could feel her quickening breath upon his cheek as their tongues fiercely mingled together, almost as one. She had to release his mouth as she gasped for air. Then she placed her right hand against her head and she moaned, screamed and shuddered uncontrollably.

He rolled her over upon her back and he was now on top of her. She drew her legs around his buttocks, helping him drive deeper inside of her. She quivered beneath him, as he started slowly and then quickened and accelerated his relentless pace. He gyrated slowly within her while he raised his body up with his arms, he propped himself on one arm, continuing to slowly rotate atop her.

He lightly began to caress her face with his fingertips. Moving his fingers around lightly touching her, outlining every feature of her face as he slowly rotated deep within her. She felt excited yet relaxed at his touch. Every nerve in her body was responding, sending pleasant sensations to her mind.

He pulled himself out of her again, causing her to gasp. He rolled her onto her belly, and mounted her from behind again. She arched her buttocks up to greet him as he entered her. He slowly closed her legs with his knees as he began to thrust deep within her still wet moistness. She arched herself up as much as she could, allowing him to penetrate deep within.

He began slowly, working her intense passion up again, and then he quickened the pace as her panting quickened also. His hands entwined with hers, as she squeezed onto his palms. He pounded unmercifully into her, deeper, harder, nonstop, pushing faster deep inside. She climaxed again, screaming out, and he felt her quiver beneath him once again. Before her tremors subsided she felt his warm liquid essence discharge inside her, as he began to shudder, screaming out her name.

They lay together within each other's arms. Her head atop his chest, as he held her tightly against his body. Each feeling content, both exhausted from their affair, yet both unable to remove the smiles from their faces. They relaxed in each other's arms, as he asked, "One more time?"

Butterfly

You're a magnificent white butterfly,
with your elbows held high;
I am a delicate tree bough,
On which you alight and kiss bye.

I am succulent cut fruit ,
Out of season from afar;
begging to be eaten,
just like a Dove bar.

You are a dancing moth glancing
and clinging to my mirror
where your image inspires you
to be nearer and clearer.

We are the intimate odors
that wrap around a bed
after two lovers have just loved
each other half dead.

If

If modesty was immoral I would free you
from your white skirt and blouse,
that border on restraint,
and let you feel the breezes that blow by
the tropics of your cancer and your capricorn.

I would strip your trappings off, one by one,
and have you be happy to be free, beloved.

I should see you in my eyes and in my hands
the glitter of the precious gem
you keep in hiding
and finger that smooth and polished pearl
that is only known as you.

Do I Remember You?

Have we ever met before?
Did I know you many years ago?
Did I meet you one summer
when every season was a lifetime
and every experience was new.
Do I remember you?

Ah, yes! You were my first love.
That summer that I shall never forget:
You were the blazing sun
and I bronzed darkly from your light;
You were warm sultry nights when I
only breathed your fragrant scent;
You were such sights and sounds
that my mind dispatched all else.

Yes, you, I remember you.
You wore silk pastel dresses
that clung to your body and sculptured you.
Or, you wore soft cottons that made you
sing and dance, sometimes sultry
and sometimes hot. I can still remember
how I longed to free you
from anything that you wore.

Yes, and I remember our first kiss!
It was a long kiss, under an oak tree
on a country road. Your lips were soft, delicate

and your taste was like sweet and fine:
enchanting. . . luscious. . . intoxicating.
I held your face in my hands
and kissed you full and strong.
I could not leave your mouth then.
And, I never have.

Yes, I remember all these days
and nights when everything was new.
Days that we spent exploring
new lands with sights and sounds
that were fairy tale places where we roamed
like children, hand in hand.
Nights that were long with each evening
spent talking and touching and loving.

Yes, the loving I remember most!
The feel of you in bed,
in each other's arms,
clinging together tightly,
is what I remember most.
Oh, what a numbing,
light-headed feeling it was!
Your scent and taste were everywhere!
They surrounded and captivated me.
We rained kisses on each other
and explored each other in every way.
I came to know each beautiful breast,
your inner thighs,
and the soft moistened hair
of your crotch . . . and all your sensitive,
secret parts within. One by one each part
was visited with tender loving touch . . .
loving, gently, gently loving.
And, when you could no longer
delay my entry, invited me in

--and we became one!

How could I forget you!
We grew together in so many,
many ways that summer:
Emotionally, physically and spiritually.
Yes, I remember you!
Yes, I remember you!

Just Below

Your slit sits just below it,
and crowns it just so;
A golden thatch,
above your snatch,
Seems to almost glow.

Your wonderful woman thighs,
open to just my size,
And clamp comfortably
around my butt.
To collect my growing prize.

We watch the mirror of it,
on top the tile while wet,
And we both share the view
of the mirror making love,
--it's like watching an erotic duet.

Limerick # 3

There once was a lady named Joan,
Who thought of the men she'd known,
While their dicks and their sizes
Would never win prizes,
They were better than beating alone.

Limerick # 4

There once was a lady admired by far,
For being mistaken for a famous porn star.
She cried, "It's all but a lie,"
Though her eyes were quite dry,
"Maybe it's 'cause I can swallow a jar!"

In A Dream

In a dream I had last night
I saw you poised above my heart
hovering, again.

As my mind cleared
(or did it cloud?)
I became aware of your scent
all around me as it aroused me
and swept into the depths of my pores
causing again the awakening of
my primal need for you.

Your body spoke to mine
in the most primitive of ways
without motion inviting me
assaulting me with its aroma of love.

I lay there feeling paralyzed,
numbed by both an aching
and a fear of you.

I was completely yours.
at your whim and mercy,
at your command and balanced
between love and lustful desire
again.

In my mind I spoke to you
and pleaded with your eyes,

"My darling, my goddess, my dream,
lay with me here; make me yours,
make me at one with you."

"You who have blessed me before
with your body and your mind,
please bless me again
and be mine
for this hour before dawn
when the world is asleep
except for us two."

"Bless me with your mouth,
your hands, and your moist cunt.
Position yourself above me
and ride me until neither of us
can move anymore."

"Then kiss me sweetly
and draw my soul into yours.
It is waiting here for you,
trembling in timid anticipation
for you."

"Oh! Caress me,
possess me completely,
and then vanish
like the spirit that you are.
But, be with me, briefly, for awhile.
I die many deaths each time you leave,
but I can only live or die with you,
my darling, my love,
my phantom lover of my dreams."

I Lay

I lay there satiated
in deepest, deepest pleasure
still wildly pulsing
from our prolonged and utter ecstasy.
How could I have ever realized
what untold secrets
you had to share.
My love, my love,
I have found my love in you,
and ecstasy I never knew
I have found them all
in you.

My Lover

You unstrap it slowly, sensually,
then move your body
away from it and let it fall.

You pull them down stirringly,
from your hips and your thighs,
step out of them and they are gone.

You are naked now, and you are my lover
--no longer working at your job,
--or someone's mother,
--or any other thing you're asked to be.

You are just my lover,
and you are just alone with me

I Saw

I saw a silhouette
of a woman
the other day
that from behind
looked like you.
She had the same
slender lines
rising along her jeans
to her sweatered spine
and a small head of hair
with large blond curls
that floated like a halo
above her head.

I never saw her face,
not wanting to leave the place
where that image sent me:
A late summer's day,
perhaps a Sunday,
when you and I
were stopped for coffee;
We were both in line,
and I was right behind,
pressing into you.
I had slipped my hand
into your denim slit
of the pocket of your jeans,

like I had just slipped my fingers
right into you.

45

I Want To Touch You There

You're lithe and long waisted,
with milky white skin,
With fine muscled limbs
that speak of the gym.

I slowly travel and explore
each separate part
Of your beautiful body
While I give you my heart.

I reach and cover your breasts
with my hands,
They meet me and blend
with my movement's demands.
"Beautiful," I tell you
and the words are not wrong.

Placing my head between your legs
That are surprisingly strong.
You twist and you show me
your peach-colored cunt
That trembles awaiting
with a glistening front.

I fumble at first,
touching everything with my tongue,

Trying to find the key that unlocks
The door that leads to when we were young.

I think I have found it,
as you let out a moan,
My nose rests on your mound
and I feel your pelvic bone.

The tip of my tongue
starts to survey and compare
The vastness of feelings
That lie within you there.

I keep up light touches,
giving your clitoris fits
While my hands keep moving
round your nipple tips.

I tease and I touch every sensitive thing,
While striving to reach
Your most important thing.

You let me roam
your body's most intimate domain,
But outside your heart
I seem to always remain.

I don't care if I reach you
everywhere elsewhere:
Please open your heart,
I want to touch you there.

Little Red

Red little pussy in my bed
Are you reddish pink or pinkish red?
Red little pussy, you must be a sight,
With all those juices gushing tonight.

Red little pussy you must be fed;
Raise both legs and make them spread.
Sucking and fucking are in store tonight,
Now do me a favor and put on the light!

Lunch

You asked me to lunch once,

it would take an hour you said.

I met you in a park,

where you placed a feast upon a spread.

I remember how you dressed;

You seemed so alive.

You wore a shift of lilac:

it brought fire to your eyes.

Our secret thoughts were stirred

by food that had no fork or spoon,

and we drank undated wine

well before noon.

You poured from the bottle

and whispered, "You're mine,

in every way and variety

that I could ever find."

We drank that cool red wine

and talked very slow;

of dirty thoughts and deeds

that caused the wine to glow.

You undressed me in your mind

and I undressed you too;

your breasts were in my hands

and you touched all that you knew.

You said to place my head

where you needed it so much;

I said I would do for you

if we could do it Dutch.

You said, "That's right, yes,

do all that you please!"

I said, "You're the best,

now open your knees!"

Cats

(These words were found written on the inside of a crumpled pro-
gram for the musical "Cats")

Why am I so lucky as to be sitting next to the most beautiful
woman I have ever met. Am I imaging all this? Am I stark raving
mad?

Or is she?

I can't concentrate on the musical for long. I keep thinking of her.
I keep thinking about what we did last night, and what we'll do tonight in just a few hours.

Oh, my!

I have my hand touching the inside of her thighs. I can feel the
softness there.   I can imagine what lies there. Dare I move my
hand up a bit? Is that older woman watching? Should I care?

I'm so aroused!

She laughs and I laugh. Her sound is sweet and happy. I'm glad.
She's had a rough week. She deserves a little happiness, and so do
I. But, do I deserve her? I think not. I will have her though, for as
long as she'll have me.

I can't wait to have her alone.

What are we seeing on the stage? Cats? All I can think of right

IRIS MEDE

now is pussy!

Limerick #5

There once was a lady with pussy of red,
Who loved giving her man plenty of head,
She said it's sweetly erotic,
And completely non-caloric,
And beats the hell out of just lying in bed.

Limerick #6

There once was a woman known as bizarre,
Because she wasn't quirky in her boudoir.
So she found herself a man,
To bite her on her can,
And left her with a great big hickey scar!

About The Author

Iris Mede And Ian Lewis

Select short story collections by the authors:

Never Let Me Feel Unloved

Many Splendors, Many Ways